Anna Katharine Green

Risifi's Daughter

A Drama

Anna Katharine Green

Risifi's Daughter
A Drama

ISBN/EAN: 9783743332126

Manufactured in Europe, USA, Canada, Australia, Japa

Cover: Foto ©Andreas Hilbeck / pixelio.de

Manufactured and distributed by brebook publishing software
(www.brebook.com)

Anna Katharine Green

Risifi's Daughter

RISIFI'S DAUGHTER

A DRAMA

BY

ANNA KATHARINE GREEN

———

NEW YORK & LONDON

G. P. PUTNAM'S SONS

The Knickerbocker Press

1887

Press of
G. P. Putnam's Sons
New York

DRAMATIS PERSONÆ.

OSALDI—A Florentine prince.

GIOVANNI, }
CAMILLO, } His sons.

RISIFI—A wealthy merchant.

ZENO—Friend and confidant of OSALDI.

LEON, }
SILVIO, } Gentlemen.

URBINO—Friend and confidant of RISIFI.

ANTONIO.

BEPPO.

PAULO.

PAGE.

PRIEST.

MESSENGER.

GINEVRA—Daughter of RISIFI.

BIANCA.

ACT I.

ACT I.

Enter OSALDI *and* GIOVANNI.

GIOVANNI.

What, gone ?   All gone ? fame, fortune, substance,
    lands ?
Nought but the title left ?

OSALDI.

         Ay, ay, nought else.
The goodly tree of our most ancient house
Which for so long a time hath stood the shock
Of every wind of heav'n, hath fall'n at last ;
And I th' unhappy cause.

GIOVANNI.

         Thou ?

OSALDI.

         But for me,
For me and that wild folly of the blood .
Which would not look on danger in the bud,
However brave to meet it in the flower,
You and your brother might have stood this day

3

Among the proudest nobles in the land,
Instead of hiding in these dim old halls
Heads that were made for council, hands for fight,
And hearts whose manly worth a father sees
But dares not praise too much, lest men should say,
" The loss of fortune, favor, and repute
Hath made the old man mad ; low as he is,
He thinks to charm the world back to his feet
With his two needy sons." Ah, my Giovanni,
You are too gentle ; you but wrench the sword
When you should boldly draw it. Wrong like this,
Demands a harsher treatment.

GIOVANNI.

                            Wrong ? Well, yes,
Perhaps it was a wrong. But when did wrong
E'er mount so high that love could not outsoar it ?
Father, I love you, and in that word toss
The past away forever. As for the future,
If we be born Osaldis, let us be
Osaldis to the core, and made to bend,
Stoop with such strength we crush the thing we
        stoop to,
And rise up lords again. You smile, my sire ;
Does my weak body put to shame my words ?
If so, my deeds must put to shame my body.

OSALDI.

If I did smile it was with pride, my boy,
To find my fledglings grown. You and your brother
Are two young eagles hatched upon a rock

But needing nought but your great eagle hearts
To teach you how to mount.   Oh that my strength
Were as my years, that I might live to see
Your wings above the clouds !

GIOVANNI.

                    You will, you will.
By this right arm's good force——

OSALDI.

                    No force, my son ;
I am too old for force.   I fain would see
The end before I die, and fortune forced,
Yields not till blood and sinew, heart and brain
Have well-nigh spent themselves.

GIOVANNI.

                    How then attain ?

OSALDI.

As you attain the fruit of yonder tree ;
Stand up and reach, my son.

GIOVANNI.

                    But all are reaching,
And what am I that I alone should pluck ?

OSALDI.

You are a prince.

GIOVANNI.

                    Ay, but you say a poor one,
And gold seeks gold.

OSALDI.

True if it seek not rank.
Boy, you are dull, methinks.   The ripest fruit
Which hangs within the reach of noble youth,
Falls but through woman's favor.   You must wed.

GIOVANNI.

Ah !

OSALDI.

For——   [*Enter* ZENO.
But hold ! here comes our worthy Zeno ;
Step back, I pray, but do not quite withdraw ;
I 'd speak to you anon.
[GIOVANNI *draws back.*   OSALDI *approaches* ZENO.
Well, well, what news ?
What says the sleek Rigoli ?

ZENO.

Good, my lord,
The worthy   count   sends   greeting ;   knows   your
     fame
And bows unto it ; knows your son's deserts
And cries himself his servant ; feels them both
Too weighty in the balance 'gainst his daughter,
And therefore must decline the brave alliance
You bade me to propose.

OSALDI.

Ay, ay, ay, ay,
A smooth, soft message, but it breaks my heart.

My fame? Great heavens! My deserts? Ye
    powers!
They are most weighty. Had we owned more gold,
Methinks we then had seen a miracle,
Since what had made all other scales weigh down
Had tossed this up in air. Ah, well, the world
Speaks suavely in this answer of Rigoli.

ZENO.

My lord, a five year hence the Count Rigoli
Will think himself much honored if he gain
So much as late admission to Osaldi.

OSALDI.

Hath Giocchi then——

ZENO.

                My gracious lord, no Giocchi;
There 's craft in Giocchi blood; I like not Giocchi.

OSALDI.

Ay, but what said he? Something blunt, I wot.
What said the jealous Giocchi?

ZENO.

                Truly, Prince,
He said no more than this: " When proud Osaldi
Can show a fortune equal to his birth,
Then let him seek my daughter.

OSALDI.

When, when, *then !*
And does he think we e'er should seek his daughter
Were we so much as by one scudo richer ?
Fie on him and his daughter !

ZENO.

Yea, my lord,
We are well rid of Giocchi.   As to Uzzi——

OSALDI.

Good ! what of Uzzi ?

ZENO.

He but stared upon me,
And waving wide the fringes of his sleeve,
Passed by without a word.

OSALDI.

And this from Uzzi !
Time was when had an Uzzi but so much
As laid his hand upon my grandsire's arm,
An hundred swords had winged them to the light
To thrust the insult back.   O we are fallen !
Our day is dead indeed.

ZENO.

Never so dead
But it will rise again.   There yet is one——

OSALDI.

Who ? who ?

ZENO.

An honorable man, my lord,
Of wealth so great, Rigoli, ay, or Giocchi,
Could not heap up bajocchi to his scudi.
One with a daughter as exceeding fair
As the Rigoli 's foul ; a woman, Prince,
As young as Giocchi's daughter, and as chaste
As Uzzi's wife is not.   And though no count—
Have you not had enough of counts, my lord ?
A man of such high-reaching, quick ambition,
That in default of wealth more merchantable,
He 'd give his very life-blood, drop by drop,
To see his daughter wedded honorably.
Ah, I have heard him talk ! no count, I say,
But yet——

OSALDI.

No count ?   Belike a noble, then,
In all but titles : simple seignior, Zeno,
But of most gentle pedigree and station.

ZENO.

No pedigree, my lord ; but patience ! tell me
Is it for names we suffer more this hour,
Or gold to make the names which we possess
As lustrous as they should be ?

OSALDI.

But this seignior ?
This brave, discreet, and most ambitious father—
What is he called, good Zeno ?

ZENO.

                    Prince, you know him ;
Risifi is his name.

OSALDI.

          A merchant ?   Heavens !
What have I done that you should mock me thus.
A merchant ! a Risifi ! O have pity !

ZENO.

My lord, it is because of my great pity
That I commend this same.   A merchant, true,
But yet a man of spotless honor also ;
No Uzzi, Prince, in this.   A merchant, true,
But yet with a most exquisite sweet daughter,
And no Rigoli here.   A merchant, yes,
But one with mind to yield his daughter up,
And in this also, neither churl nor Giocchi.
My lord, if you do wed your son to her,
You 'll live to see three counts below your knee,
And those are——

OSALDI.

          Hold ! this daughter, have you seen her ?

ZENO.

Yea, I have seen her.

OSALDI.

                    Is she merchant too ?
Are barter, bales, and commerce writ upon her ;
Shows she her blood, good Zeno ?

ZENO.

Just so much
As the rich rose shows it is born of briers ;
She is most lovely, Prince.

OSALDI.

And young, you say?

ZENO.

Scarce sixteen, yet, my lord.

OSALDI.

And chaste ?

ZENO.

Ah, Prince,
She wears her spirit plainly on her brow,
A white star in a cloudless firmament.

OSALDI.

Hum ! and a merchant's daughter !

ZENO.

Virtue, Prince,
Doth need no pedigree to make it lovely.

OSALDI.

Nor gold, it seems.   Ah, ah, and must it be ?
Must Ugo, mighty Ugo lend his blood
To make Risifi great.   It is too much.   [*A pause.*
Zeno, the storm blows heavy on Osaldi
And we must bend or break.   If I were now

A two score younger, I would cry, " Blow on
And break us if thou can'st ; we will not stoop."
But I am old ; my sons, my two brave sons
Sit heavy at my heart, and so we bend ;
May Heav'n make light the storm o'erwhelming us !

ZENO.

It will, my lord, it will.   O joyful day !
O happy, happy day !   O most kind day !   [*Exit.*

OSALDI, *bitterly.*

Ah, happy day indeed !   [*To* GIOVANNI.]

                    Son, by your leave,
Another word with you.   Touching that matter
We were engaged upon, if you do wed,
'T is certain you must wed a girl of dower ;
Is it not so ?

GIOVANNI.

        In truth it seems so, father.

OSALDI.

A girl of goodly dower ; of wealth enough
To build our old house up unto the height
Of its late grandeur ?

GIOVANNI.

            Certain, if possible.

OSALDI.

Son, it is possible.   Indeed, to tell you truly,
I know of such a one.   A fair girl too,
Of beauty most bewitching, and though lacking
In much that an Osaldi might desire,
Possessing to the full the two great needs
Of loveliness and riches.   Can you trust me ?

GIOVANNI.

Trust you !

OSALDI.

Hold ! you would ask if she is born
Of a right noble race?   Son, she is not ;
But lions crouch, and so may an Osaldi,
If, like the lion, he rouse him with a spring.

GIOVANNI.

Her name, father—her name ?

OSALDI, *embarrassed.*

Her name, my son ?
Her name ?   Why ask !   'T will be Osaldi soon.
Nay, then ; her name ?   It is—it is Risifi,
An honest one enough.

GIOVANNI.

The merchant's daughter ?

OSALDI.

How ! do you start at that ?   Are you so proud ?

GIOVANNI.

No, no, not proud. I was but thinking, father,
How base a thing it is for one who hoped
To walk above all earthly littleness,
To lead a trusting woman to the altar
Just for the gold she brings.

OSALDI.

                          But gold brings power,
And power brings honor ; you will sit on thrones
With riches for your bride ; is that so base ?
Boy, you are young, and look on life as yet
From a mere hillock's top.   To you the future
Is but the present's dim continuance,
And change a thing of circumstance, not self,
Whereas self changes soonest.   What to-day
Seems to your youth the only good in life
Will be, a five year hence, a cause of laughter,
If not of secret shame and stern repentance.
Life is no plain, however vast or varied,
But rising ground, where every forward step
Shifts the horizon.   Then be wise, my son,
And whilst you plan the present, O remember
The manhood that will tower in the future,
And give it room, room, room.   And now no more ;
I go to plead with all the saints for thee,
And a fair issue to our large endeavors.
Keep counsel till we meet, and then I look
To see thee smile again, for on thy smile
A father's pleasure hangs ; a father true,

Who did thee once a wrong, but who in this
Seeks for that wrong to make due recompense.

[*Exit.*

GIOVANNI.

So, so, thus does Giovanni seal his fate,
Like all his race before him. Is it well?
Alas, 't is not for me to question it. [*A pause.*
And thou, sweet image, which, though seen but
      once,
Hath ever dwelt within Giovanni's breast
As type of earth's supremest loveliness ;
Thou who with one unconscious glance hath made
A garden to blow ever in my thoughts ;
Must I then give thee up ; forego the hope
I scarcely knew was hope until I felt
The wreck it made in crumbling into ruin ;
Toss from my soul the one pure joy it held
Untarnished from the world, and bowing down
My head unto the yoke of ancient custom,
See all that makes life blessèd float away
With that one dream which formed my happiness ?
Yes ; for the sake of these I love so well,
My white-haired sire and him who calls me
      brother,
This, and much more, must I, Giovanni, do :
May Heaven receive the willing sacrifice !

ACT II.

ACT II.

SCENE—*Large hall in the Osaldi palace.*

Enter LEON *and* SILVIO, *meeting.*

LEON.

What 's this? What 's this? Defiance from the
    south,
And Florence filled with rumors of a war?

SILVIO.

So Beppo says, a man more slow to prick
The gusty bags of rumor, than to act
Upon th' event when it calls out for action.

LEON.

'T is news to rouse Osaldi and awake
The slumbering lion in Giovanni's breast.

SILVIO.

Look where he comes, brows bent and eyes cast
    down
As though Ambition with its glowing wand
Had stirred his humors up.

[*Enter* GIOVANNI.

19

SILVIO, *starting forward.*

Giovanni!   Count!

LEON, *detaining* SILVIO.

Stay, man, the hawk 's in flight, let him soar on
Unstayed by thee.

SILVIO, *going.*

Then here 's for lower game.
Alphonso waits within the antechamber ;
Let us to him.

LEON.

Good! I am with you there.

[*Exeunt* LEON *and* SILVIO.

GIOVANNI.

Where is the empty sphere, my home ?
Where is the will to measure will against ;
The rocks to wear to sands with my flood waves ?
Ah, if—stupendous if !—a war were near
Hot with the smoke of conflict ; if the wind
Were blowing that should bear demanding cries
For strength and valor ; if the so small cloud
That now is sailing upward from the south
Should grow—Then woe and woe again—and yet,
Proud inward giant, lion-souled Ambition,
Thou 'dst have thy freedom then. Woe! Yet my
        soul
Could hurtle 'gainst such woe and strike a flame
Of lightning out. Ah, if the cannon shook

The ground beneath men's feet ; if glare were death
And men were hurrying from this world in crowds,
Then could I rise upon the reeking field
And shake dilatingly my power out
In face of those white brows. If need should
    come—
If trembling quailing, halting, veering—men
Drew back from vict'ry side by side with Death,
Then I—
        Ah, old Thermopylæ ! thy Shades
White, crowned and smiling as they smiled in death,
Pass nigh and fill my breast with jealous shame
That I can stretch no brother-hand to such !
Ah, warrior-creating Marathon !
That drew from clay great hero-souls, put sword
In hand of Pleasure, pricked young men to deeds
Which shake the world e'en now ! Ah, Hannibal,
Surrounded by thy long-haired heroines !
O Crecy ! Agincourt ! and fields
Where ev'n the grass that blooms grows quiveringly
In pride of showing where a hero died !
I 'm one of you, O warriors, and my feet
Go ever wandering towards a battle-field.
                [*The castle bell rings.*
Ha ! what is that ?   [*Shouts within.*
        [*Enter* LEON, *followed by others.*
        How now, what means this noise ?

LEON.

'T is war's alarm ! revolt is in the south
And the Duke calls for soldiers.

GIOVANNI.

           War? You mock me.
Events rush not so close upon our wish,
Else were we gods and circumstance our vassal.
The soldier-steel that buckles to my side
Hath shook its music in your ears and lo !
You cry out *War !* in echo.

LEON.

           No ; my cry
Is single and most true.   From south and east
Swells the loud call.   Although the wind be low,
There 's import in it.   In a few hours hence
Osaldi's towers will shiver in its blast
And his deep donjons tremble.

GIOVANNI.

           Welcome to it !
So it shake ruin from our walls and ope
A way to wealth without the aid of woman.
But look, the Prince.

           [*Enter* PRINCE.

LEON.

           We will remain no longer.
    [*Exeunt* LEON *and his companions.*

GIOVANNI, *kneeling.*

Father, your blessing ! In yon clarion cry
I hear a call worthy Osaldi's answer.
Bless me and let me go.

OSALDI.

Hath thy young blood
Leaped to the call so quick ?

GIOVANNI.

Yea, as the echo
Answers the huntsman's horn.

OSALDI.

'T is well ; but son,
A man of princely blood goes not to war
With his own sword alone.   You must have men,
And men means gold, and gold means——

GIOVANNI.

Marriage ?

OSALDI.

Yes.

GIOVANNI.

Oh, I had hoped the heavens had turned the scale
Against that hard alternative.   But fate
Wills not to man both fame and happiness :
He who would rest his daring foot on heights
So single and so lofty, ev'n must learn
To tread his own heart down.

OSALDI.

And you consent ?

GIOVANNI.

At once, so this, as all things, speed me hence
Unto the field of war.

OSALDI.

It shall, or nought
Shall be by us concluded.   Zeno, good friend,
A mission for your wisdom.

[*Enter* ZENO.

How! your frowns
Speak of fresh tidings.   Well, what now? what
    now?

ZENO.

A delegation, Prince ; a line of guests
Drawn up before the gate in order soldierly ;
A goodly company.

OSALDI.

Their names ? condition ?

ZENO.

Worthy their errand, if not worthy thee.
Rigoli, master, Giocchi, and proud Uzzi,
In all the pomp of retinue and horse.

OSALDI.

Ha, the three foes most deadly to our pride,
And seated at our gates !   Well, let them sit.
'T is not to wed their daughters to my sons
I warrant they have brought their insolent state
To mock my house's poverty.   Let them sit !

Long rank has made us patient ; we will see
If their new honors bide the bit as well.

ZENO.

But, Prince, they bear the symbol of the Duke.
Not petty counties, but all Florence speaks
In their shrill trumps.

OSALDI.

So, so, as War's solicitors they come ;
'T is insolence, but we 'll meet it. Friend, your ear.
Away to the Risifi ; give him hope
Of our alliance : bring us pledge of his,
And let the whole be done within the moment
As fast as horse can spring or wish can travel.
Exit [ZENO.
O we will meet these upstarts, we will meet them !

GIOVANNI.

The trumps grow clamorous.

OSALDI.

It is music, boy,
Long known to these high walls.   Let it sing on.
A past like ours commands the present's patience.

GIOVANNI.

And yet for courtesy.

OSALDI.

Hath ruin courtesy ?
Methought that ruin had no grace but pride.

Yet since 't is Florence speaks, hence to the gates
And bid the strangers welcome in the name
Of Country and the Duke.   But first your arm
Unto my chair of state.   Whate'er betides,
The single seat this room contains, holds *me.*

> [*Seats himself.*
> [*Exit* GIOVANNI.

Ah, I will show these nobles of a day
What stuff is in the man they seek to trample.

Enter GIOVANNI, *ushering in* RIGOLI, UZZI, *and*
GIOCCHI *with their suites.*

RIGOLI.

Greeting, my lord !   Rigoli stands, your servant.

OSALDI.

'T is well, Rigoli.   Thus hath your sire stood,
And your sire's sire before you. Yours too, Giocchi ;
And yours still more, proud Uzzi.

UZZI.

>   Sooth, my lord,
One needs must stand in halls where seats are
     lacking.

GIOCCHI.

And cry himself your servant whom the Duke
Honors with his commands.

OSALDI.

>   So, so, the Duke.
Your courtesy, my lords, outsoars my thanks

And puts my age to blush. Before such wit
My threescore ten may well bow down its head
And yield its seat unquestioning.   [*Rises.*
                    Your wishes, seigniors ;
In deference to the Duke, I stand to listen.

UZZI.

'T is well ; the Duke shall know your complaisance;
'T will please him, doubtless.

OSALDI.

                Come ! your message, counts.

RIGOLI.

It is of war. Our lord Duke goes to war
With all his chivalry. You have two sons ?

OSALDI.

Ay, ay.

RIGOLI.

            Two sons of such an ancient house
Should shed a beacon-light upon the field,
Or so the good Duke thinks. Could you then
    spare
Their youth to the fair cause—

OSALDI.

                    Well, well ?

RIGOLI.

                        The Duke
Would greet them with all honor, them and theirs—

A hundred men accoutered to the full
Were company sufficient—give them place
And generalship ; for even youth hath claims
When fivescore men come pricking at their heels.
And furthermore, the good Duke bids us say,
That for the loan of such fair sums as you
May in your wisdom deem commensurate
With your past fame and present consequence,
He shares with you in fairness such results
As wait upon the enterprise.
Such is our message ; may your answer to it
Be like your state : all substance if no show.
                                    [*All bow mockingly.*

OSALDI, *aside.*

Now may the saints grant patience !
                              Counts, my state
Greets with indulgence your conspicuous effort
At unaccustomed duties.   May the years
Bring you more aptitude.   As for your message,
It doeth honor to the Duke and me ;
My answer to it—[*aside to* GIOVANNI] See if Zeno
    comes !
[*To Counts*] I will consider.   [*Aside*] O to haste
    him hither !

GIOCCHI.

Stay ! hear Rigoli out.

OSALDI.

            What ! is there *more ?*

RIGOLI.

No more than this : that if as gossip prates
The means are lacking to my lord the Prince
To meet the hour's demands in manner fitting
To his great name and famous heritage,
The good Duke shows his mercy, and remem-
b'ring
The loneliness of age, entreats of thee
To keep thy hearthstone merry with thy sons,
Since they are all that wretched fortune leaves
thee.

OSALDI.

Ah, ah, the Duke is kind and ye are kind.
That look of decent shame and trembling awe
Becomes your faces bravely. Thanks, my lords ;
Ruin, were ruin mine, would find a balm
In such display of grateful sympathy.

               [They bow mockingly.

GIOVANNI, *aside to* OSALDI.

Have patience, father ; malice tips their scorn.

OSALDI, *aside to* GIOVANNI.

Patience? Oh, ay ; such as the lion hath
That leaps in thought with every burning throb
Of his hot heart against the bars that cage him.
No sign of Zeno yet ?

GIOVANNI.

        None yet, my lord.

GIOCCHI.

So, Prince, you understand us?

OSALDI.

Ay, too well.
Reverence and awe are easy read, my lords,
So are servility and slavish fear.
My grandsire Ugo read them plain enow
Upon the faces of your ancestors.
But come, enough of this.   The Duke's command
Awaits its answer.   Let us—[*Aside*] Ha, the sound
And clatter of a horse within the court.   [*To* Gio-
vanni.]
Is 't Zeno?   quick!   who waits without there?
speak!

GIOVANNI.

Zeno, my lord.

OSALDI *to* GIOVANNI.

Good!   Bid him give you straight
The answer that he brings me.   Note it, thou;
And if it pleasure you, if fate has smiled,
And the Risifi cries Amen! to us,
Lift up your head on entering; but if No,
Bow down your neck as God bows down our house
Beneath the scornful heel of fortune's upstarts.
[*Exit* GIOVANNI.

RIGOLI, *apart to* UZZI.

I know not why, but I like not his looks;
Should he deceive us, we should show some small.

UZZI, *apart to* RIGOLI.

It cannot be.   Did 'st mark the rats our steps
Scared from the arras?   They were lean, my lord ;
Lean rats bespeak scant larders.

RIGOLI *apart to* GIOCCHI.

And proud looks,
A store of hidden ducats.

GIOCCHI *apart to* RIGOLI.

Do not think it.
Watch how he trembles, how his old head sinks
With less and lesser hope upon his breast.
No ducats there, good friends.

OSALDI, *with effort, his eyes fixed on the door.*

My noble seigniors,
The hour has come to answer.   Tell the Duke
That the Osaldis' fortunes have not kept
Strict pace with their desires.   Time was when word
Like this from the good Duke had met response
As thunder follows lightning.   But years and folly,
Love, and the calls of war, have pricked our coffers,
And they stand somewhat drained.   We—[*with
    greater effort*] are   poor—[*Door opens,* GIO-
    VANNI *enters, head erect.* OSALDI'S *voice
    rings out.*]

Ay as ye guessed, my lords.   To the demand
Of the great Duke for soldiers, we can send
But thrice a hundred, duly armed and mounted,

Instead of the five thousand he had thought
Consonant with our greatness.   As for money—
Ten thousand scudi paid at once in full,
Must meekly ask indulgence of the Duke
For the round fifty we had hoped to send him.
Is it enow to give my sons a place
In front of danger?

RIGOLI, *embarrassed.*

Quite enow, my lord.
[*Aside*] The old fox *has* deceived us.

GIOCCHI.

Noble prince,
Florence owns you its debtor.   For this gift
Accept our thanks and our most humble service.
Giocchi salutes you.

RIGOLI.

And Rigoli.

OSALDI.

Good my lords,
For this same bending of your haughty necks
My purse returns you suitable reverence.

RIGOLI.

His pride o'erwhelms us ; let us hence at once.
Farewell, Osaldi ; your sons we meet anon.
[*Is about to pass, but pauses and looks back.*
As for the matter of my daughter, Prince—

OSALDI.

My lord, the jest was answered. My deserts,
Ay, and my fame,—small as it is,—you say,
Lift us above your daughter. It is well ;
I would not add to your humility ;
Speak of the thing no more. [RIGOLI *passes on.*

UZZI.

Uzzi departs,
But not without repentance. Should my lord
Still wish to wed his son unto my daughter—

OSALDI.

Uzzi might pause. Pass on, pass on, my lord,
We need you not. Upon your crookèd soul
Repentance sits askew.

GIOCCHI.

Take Giocchi's farewell.
As for the lightness of our seeming scorn,
Accept the sorrow of our better nature,
And speak not of our folly to the Duke.

OSALDI.

I am Osaldi, seignior, and not Giocchi ;
I never speak of folly. Hence ! away !

ACT III.

ACT III.

SCENE I.—*A room in the Osaldi palace.*

Enter GIOVANNI *and* ZENO.

GIOVANNI.

You say she 's fair.

ZENO.

           Most fair ; her innocent face
Hath that sweet look which comes from gentle
    thoughts,
And in the glance of her large, lucent eye
A witchery dwells that many a princely dame
Would give her ancient pedigree to add
Unto her store of charms.   O you will love her
When you shall see her.

GIOVANNI.

           Think you so, good Zeno ?
A heart like mine springs not at bliss so lightly.
If kindness starts unbidden in my breast
At touch of her soft spirit, it is all
My anxious soul dare hope.   But to th' affair
For which we 've met.   As matters look to-day
'T is time I saw and swore allegiance to

37

This fair bewitchment, lest the call to war
Come e'er our force and armament be ready.

ZENO.

So thinks the noble Prince, and so, Risifi ;
Wherefore it chances that on Agnes' eve
The lordly merchant throws his portals wide
For your betrothal.

GIOVANNI.

Agnes' eve ?   'T is soon.

ZENO.

Meantime your father prays that all be kept
Secret as heretofore.   Your brother—

GIOVANNI.

Well?

ZENO.

Comes from the hunt to-day.   See that he smiles
In happy ignorance of what his youth
May deem a degradation to his name,
Till the event be certain and his scorn
Fall pointless on the fixèd shield of fate.

GIOVANNI.

Unwelcome tidings are as restless, seignior,
As untrained falcons, and will fly, I ween,
Whether we will or no.

ZENO.

Not if the jess
Be strong and the hand steady.

GIOVANNI.
　　　　　　　　　Well, well, well.
　　　　　　　　　　[*Exit* ZENO.
So, so! but three days now, and honor, wealth,
The pomp of generalship, and pride of power
Will be my own, and life be set at last
Within the groove of action. 'T is an end
Towards which my thoughts have run since
　　youth took on
Color from high ambition ; yet, alas !
Where is the joy with which I looked to see
This hour of triumph crowned? Gone with the
　　love
That flushed the arid mountain tops of fame
With lustre not their own. Thus runs the life
Of man towards disappointment. To be great,
Fits not with to be happy. Ah, base wretch,
Who would have all or none ; what, then, is love?
A dream, a flitting dream. Shall the ship pause
Because the breath of orange-groves comes sweet
From some near siren isle ? What says my sire,
A man whose heart for threescore years and ten
Hath run the gamut of earth's joys and sorrows,
And touched its every chord : "In man's short
　　span
He runs on many a hope. To-day 't is love
That seems his only good ; to-morrow, knowledge ;
A five year hence, pow'r and the chance to wield it ;
A decade later all his thought is profit ;
Then comes old age, and with it joys of ease,
And life again in his posterity."

It is the voice of wisdom, but alas !
What youth e'er gave it heed without the aid
Of harsh experience.   *[A pause.*
                    Ah, what is life !
'T is but a passing touch upon the world ;
A print upon the beaches of the earth
Next flowing wave will wash away ; a mark
That something passed ; a shadow on a wall,
While looking for the substance, shade departs ;
A drop from the vast spirit-cloud of God
That rounds upon a stock, a stone, a leaf,
A moment, then exhales again to God.

Enter CAMILLO, *singing.*

My lady sits at her casement ;
O heav'n, how fair, how fair !
The jessamine vines about her
Make halo round her hair :
I see, and longing, lift in singing
The joy and pain within me springing.

My lady smiles from her casement ;
She plucks a flow'r and stands,
Holding it close to her bosom
In two white tremulous hands :
The songs I sing leap high and higher,
Pleading like hungry flames of fire.

My lady leans from her casement ;
The flow'r has felt her kiss ;
Body and soul I kneel to meet it,

The moment heaves with bliss,
When lo ! she speaks, and " Love, to thee,"
She whispers, " far away on sea,
This kiss, and this, and this."

GIOVANNI.

Brother, your mood is merry.

CAMILLO.

Sooth, why not ?
Does not the sun shine ?   Do I not fare well ?
And have not all the prettiest girls in Florence
Smiled on me from their casements ?   Tut, Gio-
    vanni,
Like our famed grandsire, you are too ambitious,
Your spirit is too broad.   The hungry sea
Hath need of all the stars to make it bright,—
A stream 's content with one.

GIOVANNI.

Ambitious ?   I ?
Well, yes, I am ambitious ; should I be
A true Osaldi else ?   The pow'r that shone
From Ugo's martial front and made our name
A trump to call all Tuscany to battle,
Is not so dead that you or I can stand
Upon the verge of war and not feel start
The fine responsive blood.   I would behold
Our father smile again, and see thee sit
High as our rank demands.

CAMILLO, *bitterly.*

Our rank !

GIOVANNI.

How now !
You sigh, Camillo, you upon whose youth
The sun has shone and pretty maidens smiled.

CAMILLO.

Sigh ?   Nay, not so, or if by chance I did,
'T was as the breezes sigh amid the blooms
Of honeyed forests.   Joy weighs hard as pain
And oft-times owns a kindred language.

GIOVANNI.

True ;
Yet now you sigh again, and if my ear
Translates the tone aright, not joy but grief
Speaks to the heart in that uneasy echo.
If sorrow's tooth has touched your gaysome youth,
It fits my love to know it.   Speak and learn
How light a grief can grow when shared by friend-
ship.

CAMILLO.

It is not much ; at least to your discretion
'T will not seem much.   I love and love in vain.
'T is a boy's grief, why note it ?

GIOVANNI.

Love ?   *You* love ?

CAMILLO.

Ay, but I said 't was nought ; spare me your mocks ;
I know 't is folly, yet man lives by love,
And folly makes the paradise of youth.

GIOVANNI.

I mock ?   And whom—But no ; to ask thee that
Were to intrude within the sacred spot
Which each man holds most chary from his fellows—
The sacred human heart : I ask not that ;
But why in vain, Camillo, why in vain ?
Beauty like yours would start a tender thought
Within a breast of stone ; why then in vain ?
Are maidens' hearts so very hard to win ?

CAMILLO.

That I know not, Giovanni ; I but know
This maid's was not if that the merriest eye
Which e'er smiled mercy to a suppliant
Spake truth in its soft language.   But, alas !
In this hard world of place and circumstance
Fate rears up other barriers to delight
Than that of love repelled.   I am no mate
For this sweet damsel, or by thy proud code
She is no mate for me.   By rank a prince,
I may not wed——

GIOVANNI.
Well, well ?

CAMILLO.

A tradesman's daughter.
Ah, I wot well you 'd start.

GIOVANNI.

If I did start
It was with wonder at the impish tricks

With which fate mocks us men. A tradesman's
    daughter !
And you can love her and esteem yourself
Rich if she smiles, and blest if you but wear
Her beauty like a jewel on your heart..
Well, well, this barrier to your rightful joy
May prove less lofty than your fears imagine.
Hast told our father ?

CAMILLO.

                    'T were an effort lost ;
I know his mind too well.

GIOVANNI.

            Yet had'st thou told him——

CAMILLO.

And heard my darling scorned ? Nay, nay ; my
    heart
Is large enough for anguish, but too small
To hug a shame within it.

GIOVANNI.

                    Humph ! and yet
You dearly love her.

CAMILLO.

            Love her ? Hear the whole.
It was a day in June, and I who prize
The song of birds and all those shy delights
That hide within the forest's bosky glens,

Above the earthlier charms of street and mart,
Was wandering in the vales without the town,
When suddenly from out their ambient shade
A creature stepped of such entrancing mien,
I felt I ne'er in all my life before
Had looked on mortal beauty.   Young she was,
And innocent as holy temples are
Whose atmosphere is worship.   Straight to knee
I sank all trembling, soul and body both
Acknowledging unwittingly their mistress ;
But of what followed it were hard to tell,
Since lapsed in joy, I scarce remember more
Than that I heard her voice and felt the clasp
Of her shy hand as from the wood's recess
I led her to her fellows.   Earth and air
Had felt the touch of heav'n, and in the shock
My dazzled spirit reeled.   Nor of that hour
When pricked to action by my love and longing
I sought those woods again, and roaming, came
Upon her musing by the streamlet's bank,
A smile like heav'n upon her innocent mouth,
And in her eyes that look which lifts the spirit
Up as on wings of light, I may not speak.
It is enough that when with late discretion
I asked her name I——

GIOVANNI.

Well ?

CAMILLO.

Knew what despair was.

GIOVANNI.

So, you forsook her?

CAMILLO.

What was left to love
Since fate and duty to our sire decreed
I could not be her husband?

GIOVANNI.

This was when?

CAMILLO.

Some seven long weeks ago. It seems a lifetime.

GIOVANNI.

And you remember?

CAMILLO.

Will I e'er forget?

GIOVANNI, *after a pause.*

Brother, your case is not so lost to hope
As it would seem.   I may not tell you more,
But if you 'll meet me at Risifi's villa
Upon the eve of blessed Agnes day,
You will yourself——

CAMILLO, *falling back.*

Risifi! then you know——

GIOVANNI.

A merchant? Yes, and, stranger still, may soon,
Be pleased to know a merchant's lovesome daughter.

CAMILLO.

What secret is there here ?

GIOVANNI.

                    Ask not, but trust
Your fate to Heav'n, and meet me as I 've said.
Grim doom holds not such clutch upon our souls,
But sometimes in this harsh, uneasy world,
Our boldest wishes meet with strange fulfilment.

SCENE II.—*A vale without Florence. Huntsmen's horns heard in the distance.*

Enter GIOVANNI *and* LEON.

GIOVANNI

'T is my last hunt. Through all the rousing din
Of you mad horns I hear the sound of trumps
Calling me hence to battle. O the joy
Of freedom to the soul that long hath lain
Behind the bars of straitening circumstance!
Scarce can I bide the hour of my release,
My heart calls so for action.

LEON.

And your bride?
The fair young maiden that awaits your troth-
    plight,
Have you no thought for her!

GIOVANNI

My bride? Ah, Leon,
My bride is fame. I have no heart to give
To fairest woman now. A shadow dwells
Where once such hopes had birth.
    [*Enter at a distance* GINEVRA, *followed by* BIANCA.
But who is this?

45

LEON.

I know not, seignior, yet her beauty shows
Triumphant in these shades. Methinks her glance
Makes the whole place to shine.

GIOVANNI.

Ah, heaven ! yes, yes.
Leon, once since her face seen thus by chance
Hath roused the passion of my manhood up,
And filled my soul with homage. Hath stern fate
Sent her this way to tempt me ? Let 's away !
I will not meet her look, her innocent look,
So tender, yet so blithe. Risifi's daughter
Hath claims upon me now that make such dreams
A sinful madness.

LEON.

What ! you love this stranger ?

GIOVANNI.

I love my honor. Let us hence, good Leon,
For me the hunt is o'er.

LEON.

And this is life !
[*Exeunt* GIOVANNI *and* LEON.

GINEVRA, *coming forward.*

I 'm weary, my Bianca, let us rest.

BIANCA.

Yes, lady, but not here.

GINEVRA.

And why not here?

BIANCA.

The place is dark. I dread the chill which breathes
From out these clustering boughs.

GINEVRA.

I feel no chill.
I love this heavy shade, this brooding gloom ;
My thoughts make light enough. I scarce could
    breathe
For rising rapture, were there sunlight too.

BIANCA.

But lady——

GINEVRA.

Nay, Bianca, cross me not.
I see no shadows here. The place to me
Is bright as summer and as sweet as June.
Rich-blooded birds and flow'rs inch-deep with
    honey
Hide in its soft recess ; while to my ears
All the wild passion of a young joy pants
In the quick tremble of its laughing leaves.

BIANCA.

And you enjoy such music ?

GINEVRA.

                    Yes ; did'st doubt it ?
Because I pinch your ears and steal your gauds
And play you tricks and laugh from morn till night,
Did'st think my spirit owned no deeper mood ?
The maddest brook that trips it through the glen
Has here and there along its joyous course
Shy resting-places for its tired foot
And spots for quiet musing.   *This* is mine :
Then leave me to my dreams.

BIANCA.

                    The girl who dreams
In bow'rs like these where not a sunbeam dwells,
Has sweetest mem'ries linked unto its gloom,
Or such bright hopes they strike a color through
Its darkest portals.   Hast such mem'ries, lady ?

GINEVRA, *startled.*

I ? Yes, in sooth, of many a gaysome hour
Spent at your side with lute or harp or book ;
What other could I have ? But how ? You start.

BIANCA.

I thought I heard a step.

GINEVRA, *singing.*

You hear the winds at antic play,
You hear the brooks sing roundelay,
The flow'rs you hear, coquetting, dear,
But not——

                    Nay, then I 'll quit my pranks,
I cannot bide your frowns.   You sigh for sunshine.
Go, then ; I 'll join you soon.

BIANCA.

                    Upon the terrace ?

GINEVRA.

Yea, on the terrace.

BIANCA.

                    Good !   I will wait thee there.
Only as you do love me, gentle lady,
Linger not here too long.   Remember, madam,
That your good father hath some words of import
To say to thee to-night.

GINEVRA.

                    I will remember.
Pray they be words of joy.

BIANCA.

                    They are indeed ;   [*Aside.*
Or should be if some wandering dream of love
Hath not made ruthless havoc with a soul
We thought as free as air.   [*Exit.*

GINEVRA.

    The good Bianca ! as little doth she reck that
happy accident hath already given to my ears the
gist of her most wonderful secret, as that this son
of the Osaldi, whom my father in his wisdom hath

seen fit to accept for my bridegroom, is that stranger to my eyes which they in their most fortunate ignorance seem to consider him. But fate is a gay trickster and plays mad pranks with us all. 'T is not the first time the untoward lifting of a curtain hath brought strange counsels to light. The young Osaldi ! Well, well, he is certainly a most exquisite gallant. His Good-day, lady, and his Good-even to you are flavored with the cream of perfectest courtesy. Then, for a Tuscan, he hath also a certain comeliness ; but have I not sworn, in good-faith too, that I would not wed a Tuscan were he the best-made man in Italy ? Then there is his glance, which proclaims to my understanding that he loves me—which same seems over-bold. But, then, his smile ! Well, for a smile it certainly does credit to his wit ; but I cannot live upon smiles, though if I could, I might consent to make a trial of his,—and starve belike for my pains. [*Muses.* *Enter* CAMILLO.

CAMILLO, aside.

She 's here, and my heart's language hath not deceived me. Now if it be true, as my brother's words seem to betoken, that love and fortune await me on St. Agnes' Eve at the house of her father, it can be no treason to my future fate to breathe forth one breath of the passion that consumes me. [*Aloud*] Lady ?   .

GINEVRA, aside.

'T is he. Now heart be still, and wit be all alert to hide my maiden shame.

CAMILLO, *aside.*

She does not hear me ; or can it be that the mockery of her spirit hath obtained mastery over her tenderness ? I must determine. [*Advances.* Fair lady, greeting ! A kiss for your sweet thoughts.

GINEVRA.

A kiss, Seignior Camillo ? That were a poor exchange for thoughts like mine ; so if it please you I will keep my thoughts and you your kiss ; and lest it should seem ungracious in me to give nothing upon your asking, I will bestow upon you my most choice Good-day, and so leave you to your meditations. [*Is about to withdraw.*

CAMILLO.

You have the true generosity, lady ; you give away what it costs you the most to part from. Nay, rumple not your lip ; it is the truth, for all your pretty poutings. Convince me it is not.

GINEVRA.

Your pardon ; but that would take words, and words would take time, and time given to one of your persuasion would refute all my arguments on the face of them.

CAMILLO.

Well, lady, since it is your pleasure to be consistent rather than happy, adieu. Had you stayed but so long as the bee pauses on an oleander blossom, you had heard——

GINEVRA.

Buzzing, seignior ?

CAMILLO.

Yes, if by that word you would denominate vows of constancy and devotion. For I do greatly love you and would tell you so.

GINEVRA.

And for that you expect me to linger ! as though vows were new to my ears and words of love as strange to my understanding as tropical birds to the eyes of a Norseman.

CAMILLO.

If you do love me you will linger.

GINEVRA.

Yet if I do, be sure it is from some other motive than love.

CAMILLO.

So it be not from hate, I am contented.

GINEVRA.

To be contented with little proves you to be a man of much virtue.

CAMILLO.

When I have you, I am content with much.

GINEVRA.

That adder is a wise insertion, seignior : it saves you from shame and me from anger. Hark ! some one comes.

CAMILLO.

'T is but the wind. It is a kindly breeze and grieves to hear a pretty maid so harsh unto her lover.

GINEVRA.

I do not own a lover, please your worship.

CAMILLO.

Then mend your poverty and accept one, lady.

GINEVRA.

I am too young to wear a jewel so pretentious.

CAMILLO.

Time is a care for youth and marriage a happy speeder of time.

GINEVRA.

But youth needs no care, and if marriage speedeth time, I 'll live a maid and die one. The days run swift enough without goading, Seignior Camillo.

CAMILLO.

But, lady——

GINEVRA.

Nay, but your tongue will outstrip time if you put not a curb upon it. I' faith, seignior, I would

not seem rude, but if in your courtesy you would
consent to woo some other maiden to-day, why, I
would strive to bear it. You are not so handsome
seignior, that one would die for you.

CAMILLO.

No, lady; but what goes to make other men's
faces fair, goes to make my heart great. The
virtue of my manhood lies in the fact that I love
you.

GINEVRA.

Faith, you are not alone in that. T is the
common fault of the gallants I find. If that is
all——

CAMILLO.

But I will always love you, ev'n to death.

GINEVRA.

I doubt it not so death come soon enough.

CAMILLO, *drawing his poniard.*

Would'st have it come here and now and so prove
me true to my word?

GINEVRA.

I am no judge, to utter the doom your presump-
tion merits.

CAMILLO.

Your looks speak doom and your sweet lips hide
a sword keener than that of justice.

GINEVRA.

Have you tried them, seignior, that you speak so
knowingly concerning them? [*Retreats.*] Your
words, methinks, are somewhat like your kisses, all
breath and no substance.

CAMILLO, *following her.*

Lady? Sweet one?   [*Enter* LEON.

LEON.

I may not rest until I learn the name and quality
of the fair maid whom my lord has so long loved
to his undoing. [*Sees* CAMILLO *and* GINEVRA.]
Ah, whom have we here? The lady by my life,
and hand in hand with a gallant. Ah, my Giovanni, well was it that you hastened hence before
this tender scene acquainted you with the reverse
of love's sweet image, bitter jealousy. But who
is the fortunate youth who hath thus stolen your
treasure? I must see his face. Good heaven! it
is Camillo! I smell trouble here.

[*Exeunt* CAMILLO *and* GINEVRA *in tender converse.*
So, so, the youth's fair face, undaunted mien,
And that address which tops his beauty off
As music completes paradise, have won
This maiden for him, and my lord knows not
That she is doubly lost him. Well, well, well!
The fair Ginevra's charms must heal the wounds
This strange event will cause him.

[*Re-enter* BIANCA.

LEON.

Your favor, lady.

BIANCA.

Seignior, and yours. I seek my youthful mistress,
The fair Ginevra, whom I left but now
Amid these shadows.

LEON.

How? What name say you?

BIANCA.

Ginevra, seignior.

LEON.

Not Risifi's daughter?

BIANCA.

The same, fair stranger.

LEON.

Trebly cursed Giovanni!

BIANCA, *startled.*

What? what?

LEON.

Madam, dost know this lady is to wed
The Count Giovanni ere another week
Passes o'er Florence?

BIANCA.

Yea, I know it;
Her sire told me this morn. But she knows
    nought.
Went she this way?

LEON.

Yea, and her lover with her.

BIANCA.

Her lover?   Oh !   [*Is about to rush away.*

LEON, *detaining her.*

Lady, a word I pray you.
Art sure she knew nought of her coming marriage
When she strayed hence ?

BIANCA.

Most sure.   Her father waits
Ev'n now to tell her.   O may Heav'n decree
That tricksy Love lie close to-day and play
No idle pranks with that gay heart of hers
Before the hour be come.   A lover, say you ?
O I have stayed too long.   [*Exit.*

LEON.

Run, run ! thy feet
Will ne'er outspeed the wingèd boy you fear !
[*Re-enter* CAMILLO.
Ah, but this youth must know he wrongs his brother
In worshipping at this merry maiden's shrine.
How speeds the day, Camillo ?   [*Advances.*

CAMILLO.

Gayly, Leon.
Joys that have quivered in the scale till now,
Have over-balanced grief.   I am a man
Crowned for all time.   The maid I love, loves me.
Wot you of greater rapture ?

LEON.

Hush, O hush !
Such words will sting you when you hear to whom
This maiden's faith belongs. She is not yours
Howe'er you love, or howsoe'er may she ;
The husband destined for her by her sire
Is not yourself, but——

CAMILLO.

Hold ! not mine, this maiden ?
O Leon, have you weighed the words of doom
You toss so lightly towards me ?

LEON.

Fully, seignior;
The fair Ginevra is no wayside flow'r
To be plucked for the liking. Pride and power
Rule o'er her sweetness and command her grace,
And little as she recks the fate that waits her,
All that she hath of charm in form and feature
Is promised hence and——

[CAMILLO *reels*, LEON *rushes forward.*
O my Camillo,
Remember you 're a man. Be not o'ercome
By youth's most common grief. The maid is fair,
But so is Bisto's daughter, so the heir   .
Of proud Colonna's house. There still are left
Others as choice as she.

CAMILLO.

Others, Leon ?
Love sees not others, Love sees but the one ;

And when that one is lost, proves false, or dies,
The charm of life, its beauty and its worth,
Fade with her from the world.

LEON.

Is love like this ?
Well were it, then, you should not seek to snatch it
From one you hold so near in your observance.

CAMILLO.

From one *I* hold so near ? What mean you, Leon ?
O God, it is not——

LEON.

Seignior !

CAMILLO.

Not Giovanni ?—
Your silence does convict you.   It is he,
My brother, my own brother.

LEON.

But none knew
You loved the maiden.

CAMILLO.

O believe it not !
Giovanni knew, else why his strict command
To meet him in Risifi's halls this eve.
Giovanni knew, and, filled with jealous pride,
Bade Hope regain her seat within my breast
That he might shame me 'fore the world and her.
O cruel spite of joy !   O selfish heart !

That, drunk with its own bliss, could rise and fling
Its triumph in my face to make me mad.
But let him look to it : I am no child ;
He bids me to the feast,—*I will be there.*   [*Going.*

LEON.

But Seignior——

CAMILLO.

Wait ; you are my faithful friend,
True as my own heart's core.   Let no man know
I died but now to youth, and hope, and love.
                                                            [*Exit.*

LEON.

He bears it ill.   His looks proclaim his vengeance.
Wert wisdom to give warning to Giovanni ?
No, that were treason.   But I 'll watch the lad,
Follow his steps, and wait upon his moods,
And be on hand to hinder any mischief.   [*Exit.*

Re-enter GINEVRA *and* BIANCA.

GINEVRA.

What words are these ? You mock me, good Bianca,
Or I have heard amiss.

BIANCA.

Not so, not so.
Your father waits but now to give you tidings
Of your betrothal to Osaldi's heir.
He whom you love is not Osaldi's heir ;
Only the heir's young brother.

GINEVRA.

And I live,
I who should die !

BIANCA.

Madam, be comforted.
If Count Giovanni show a lesser grace
Than the young gallant who has won your heart,
He still is called a lordly gentleman,
Noble and kind.   A night of sober thought
Will blast this transient fancy in your breast
And fit you for your fate.

GINEVRA.

Never ! I feel it.
These fancies, as you style them, my Bianca,
That blossom to the heavens in a moment,
Strike root as deep as is despair itself,
In such a heart as mine.   'T will take a wrench
Vigorous as that which twists the life-strings free
To tear it hence.   No pow'r save that of Heav'n
Can e'er undo what this one hour has done,
Alas, alas the hour !

BIANCA.

Yet rest thee, lady.
Who knows ; perchance thy father yet may please
To grant thee thy desire.   Is not Camillo
Of blood as truly noble as his brother ?
And is not your most honorable father
Tender of her he loves ?

GINEVRA.

Ay, to a point,
But he 'll ne'er brook a folly.   To the wife
Of Count Giovanni, heir to princely titles,
He 'd give his heart for food ; but to the girl
Who dared to cross his lifetime's one ambition,
He 'd be as cruel as the Roman lord   ˙
Who stabbed his daughter to her shuddering heart
To save her from dishonor.

BIANCA.

Then, fair lady,
Since this is so, 't were surely wisdom's part
To take the fate which kindly Heav'n sends you,
Prompt to accept its good.   Too often, madam,
We scorn the cup pressed iron-like to our lips,
Which, if once tasted, would be found to teem
With wine of heavenliest vintage.

GINEVRA.
Not this cup, Bianca.

BIANCA.

You have not tasted it.

GINEVRA.
I know, I know.

BIANCA.

Take courage, lady ; think that duty bears
Perennial sweets, while joy blooms for a day.

GINEVRA.

I will, Bianca. Upon Duty, then,
I fix my constant faith ; and since it runs
Counter to joy, why, farewell youth's glad hopes ;
Farewell the merry heart and laughing brow ;
I have another business in this world
Than to link hands with Pleasure.   [*Exeunt*

ACT IV.

ACT IV.

SCENE—*Vast hall in the Risifi villa. Pages within.*
Enter ANTONIO.

ANTONIO.

Are all the candles lit ?   Are the musicians ready ?
Is every thing in train ?   The curtains—hang they
fair ?   Look to them, you, and hark you, sirrah, if
I hear anon of so much lacking as a single candle,
I will see you all beat from this hall to the street,
before sunrising.   I would have this day remem-
bered here in Florence, and by my steward's wand
it shall be, or let me never feast another prince in
rich Risifi's villa.   [*Enter* PAULO.
So you are come at last.   What say you, man,
Are all things well disposed ?   Think you these rooms
Will bear inspection ?   Is there finish here ?
A prince's eye is critical.   What say you, then ;
Look we like lords or no ?

PAULO.

                              Too much like lords
And much too little like the men we are.
Pah ! this display is odious.

ANTONIO.

How ? how ? how ?
What is amiss ?   Do you not like these hangings ?
They are the costliest to be found in Florence ;
I hope they 're not amiss.

PAULO.

They are too new ;
They smell too rank of the loom.

ANTONIO.

And yet they 're scented ;
I had the choicest odors flung upon them,
Where is your nose, man ?

PAULO.

In its place, Antonio ;
Not flung half way in air like some I wot of.
If you would save the lintels to the doors
Lower your crest a space.   A man would think
The crowns of all broad Europe had been piled
One on the other o'er that brow of yours,
In toppling insecurity.

PAGE.

Is your new doublet
Too narrow for your stomach that you puff so ?

ANTONIO.

Boy, to the scullions !   Do you criticise
The man who caters to a noble prince ?

As for you, Paulo, were it not indeed
That you 're a poor lean man unworthy greatness,
We 'd measure swords for this.

PAULO.

   Peace, peace, Antonio ;
Doublets of such rare precious stuff as thine
Are never strong.

ANTONIO.

   How ? how ? not strong, my doublet ?
He said my doublet ; here, you sirrah, you,
Am I in trim ? What folly 't is in man
To huff at a fool's babbling.
    [Page stumbles by with wine.
   Heav'ns, what damage now ?

PAGE.

Truth, good Antonio, if I might so speak,
You wear your feet too large.

ANTONIO.

   My feet ? too large ?
You say too large ? What think you now, young
  sirrah ?
Are they too large for this and this and this ?
     [Kicks him.

PAGE.

O ! O ! O ! O ! much too large : much, much,
 much !   *[Exeunt.*

Enter RISIFI, OSALDI, GIOVANNI, URBINO, ZENO,
        and LEON.

OSALDI.

Seignior Risifi, to my mind this thing
Shows but one face and that is, business, business.
You give us gold, we give you rank, 't is done,
The compact 's sealed, and compliment is useless.

RISIFI.

My lord, I would not weary you with words,
But you mistake me here.   Not as a churl,
But as a host I offer you my welcome,
Which as a guest you may receive, my lord,
And never stoop were you the Duke himself.
I never vaunt me of my bargains, Prince,
Merchantman though I be.   To a Risifi
Success is boast enough ; the world is quick
To spy out facts without a pointing finger,
And this thing is a fact.   Albeit a trader,
I am as proud as any peer in Florence ;
Let my lord rest content.

OSALDI.

                Seignior, your wisdom
Puts my old age to shame.   Henceforth behold
A prince of ancient lineage and fame
Who sees his son, the heir to all his honors,
Wed a Risifi and forbears to boast it.

RISIFI.

My lord says well ; 't is not a thing to boast of. .
Dost think to ruffle me ?   Do you not see

The more you stand upon your rank, my lord,
The more I mount and mount ?   Disdain my gold
And scoff at him who sells his best for it,
Not at the man who gives what you despise,
To win the thing you hold in noblest favor.

OSALDI.

Seignior, as guest, I would refrain from answering
Wit so acute.   Zeno, your arm.

URBINO, *aside to* RISIFI.

Good master,
Rouse not the old man's wrath too far, I pray,
Lest he should break with you.

RISIFI, *aside to* URBINO.

He 'd break his old heart
first.

ZENO, *aside to* OSALDI.

Wake not the slumbering tiger in his eye ;
'T is much too calm for safety.

OSALDI, *aside to* ZENO.

Never fear it.
The man who 's touched the goal of his desire
Quits not his hold so easy.

ZENO.

Prince, the lady !

URBINO.

The lady, seigniors !
[*Enter* GINEVRA, *attended by* BIANCA *and other ladies.*

GIOVANNI, *falling back.*

Saints of Heav'n !

LEON.

How now, what moves you so ?

GIOVANNI.

'T is she, my life's sole love,
The fair sweet woman, who, though seen but once,
Has, like a violet nestling in the shade,
Bloomed in my constant memory.   O boon
Unhoped, unlooked for !   Gift of gracious Heav'n
Where I expected nought !   But thus it is ;
We pluck at roses and encounter thorns ;
Clutch at life's thorns, and fill our hands with roses.

RISIFI.

Seignior Giovanni, in this simple maid
You see my hope, my joy, my wealth, my pride :
The one fair pearl dropped in my bosom's core
By the rude wave that wrecked her gentle mother.
You 'll find her pure and, though yet timorous,
As duteous and as tender to your suit
As fits her state of youthful modesty
And years of unstained thought.   Daughter, your
    hand
Unto my lord !

GIOVANNI.

Madam, my service to you !
In saying more, methinks I should say less ;

Before so gracious and so rare a presence
Compliment must e'er stand dumb.

GINEVRA.

               Seignior, I thank you.
However small of wit to twist fair sense
From unaccustomed words, I see in these
Your kindness and your truth.

GIOVANNI.

              Thy thanks, sweet lady,
Make music in a bosom heretofore
Unused to so divine a melody.

LEON *to* BIANCA.

She is a lovesome creature, but her face
Hath hints of sorrow shadowing its bloom,
Strange to behold in one so young and blithesome.

BIANCA.

Those who have lost their mothers unbetimes,
Oft show these sad lines in their faces, seignior ;
'T is nature's mark that life's most precious boon
Hath somehow missed them.

LEON.

               So, if not
The sign of present grief, I am content.
The count is not a man whose nuptial cup
Should hold one drop of secret bitterness.

BIANCA.

Is he so kind ?

LEON.

                   The prince of gentlemen,
Surpassed in mind by few, in worth by none ;
In manner only by the blither grace
Of his young brother. Were I lord of realms
To which one well-beloved child were heir,
I 'd ask of Heav'n no nobler husband for her
Than our Giovanni.

BIANCA.

               You speak strongly ;
May her young graces equal your desire.

GIOVANNI *to* GINEVRA.

Lady, I would not startle your sweet soul
Into a sudden passion. Not the wind
But the soft sunshine best constrains the bud
To ope its delicate leaves. Of all the words
Of gentle courtesy and deep regard.
With which I come full laden to your side,
I will but proffer one. Accept this, dear,
The choicest of my store, the rose of speech,
The sweet, *I love you,* which has been the gem
Of every language since the first fond hour
That woman's smile became a good man's heaven.

GINEVRA.

I am a plain man's daughter and scarce know
What words are meet for him who shows such grace
To one so far unworthy. But this love
Springing so quickly up at duty's call——

GIOVANNI.

So quickly ?   Ah, 't is true you know not yet
Aught of what gives to this betrothal hour
Its true significance.   Not at duty's beck,
But in despite of duty, will, and time
Have I your gentle image cherished here
Within my heart of hearts.   But, lady, hark !
The sound of music welling through the dance
Dreams in the air like perfume hanging rapt
Above its bed of bloom.   If you will tread
The coming measure, I will ease my soul
Of its one secret.

GINEVRA.

Ah, and *thou* hast one.

[*They pass on.*   RISIFI *and* PRINCE *advance.*

RISIFI.

Look where the count and my young daughter go,
With heads bent low like corn in harvest time.
What say you, Prince, if I read rightly there
This thing to them is aught but business, business.

OSALDI.

Seignior, my son is kind.   [*Draws off with* ZENO.
                    Too kind, by Heaven !
I like not yonder romance of soft looks,
Low cooing murmurs and love-sick devotion,
It suits not with our name.   I 'd have him wed her,
But love her ! 't is plebeian.   Never yet
Hath an Osaldi stooped to love a trades-girl.

ZENO.

Yet is she a rare blossom, noble Prince.

OSALDI.

Indeed I hope it. Would you have a man
Stoop to the dust and not pick up a jewel ?
[*They pass on. Enter numerous guests, among
them* ANTONIO *and* PAULO.]

ANTONIO.

It takes a great heart to forgive, they say ;
And why should I hang back ? There, man, my
hand.

PAULO.

What means the cockatoo ? I came not here
To prattle with a fool, but to behold
For once a man of mark. Where is the Prince ?

ANTONIO.

May Heav'n ordain he 's safer than thy manners,
Or he were lost indeed. Stay, is that he ?

PAULO.

Yon prancing, dancing jack-a-napes in yellow ?
O certain by the rood, the Prince, indeed,
If not Risifi's tapster.

ANTONIO.

Now in good sooth
It is Risifi's tapster. By my soul,

But you have eyes, my Paulo ;—not that mine
Are not right serviceable and trusty servants ·
Look at them else.

PAGE.

I know he has good eyes, for he has kicked me
And never missed the spot.

CONRADO, *pointing out* CLAUDO.

Stay, here 's the Prince !

ANTONIO, *advancing*.

Good Prince, most noble, great, and generous
    Prince,
Your servant, Prince !

CLAUDO.

Who is this fool ?

ANTONIO.

Fool ? fool ?

PAULO.

Easy, Antonio, this is Seignior Claudo,
The city goldsmith.

ANTONIO.

Then the word is pat.

He a prince, he ! A simple scullion boy
Might have known better had he seen thy face,
Good master Claudo.

PAULO.

Hush ! the Prince indeed.

[*Points out* BEPPO.

ANTONIO.

What ! yon poor rail without a gewgaw on him ?
Yon peakèd, plain, scrimped man in leaden hose ?
If I were born so small I 'd hang myself
But I would get more flesh.
      [*Advances to* BEPPO, *saluting him profoundly.*

                    My gracious Prince !
Your servant, Prince. Doth my lord Prince need
    aught ?
Are all his wants considerèd and supplied ?

BEPPO, *lending himself to the joke.*

How ! is this Antonio, my good Antonio,
Chief caterer of Florence and the rightful lord
Of this rare feast ?

ANTONIO, *bowing still deeper.*

            My lord, you do me honor.
[*Aside.*] Where are yon rascals ? They are ever
    off
When a man gets his due. [*Aloud*] My lord, your
    will ?
I hope my lord is satisfied with all ?

BEPPO.

Um ! so, so. You have done fairly if so be
The wine is somewhat sour.

ANTONIO.

           The wine—sour ? sour ?

You surely jest, my lord.   The wine ?   How now,
What mean you, sirrahs, hanging 'bout me thus ?
Off to your duties, off !

BEPPO.

                    The fruits are good,
Though something scarce.

ANTONIO.

Good heavens !
                    [*To* PAULO *and the others.*
                    What ? about me still ?
Have you nought else to do but eye my lord ?
Away ! the noble Prince and I would converse.

BEPPO.

These hangings, as I take it, were put up
Not at thy own suggestion.   They 're too gay
For taste refined as thine.

ANTONIO.

                    True, but Risifi
Is sovereign here.   He would have yellow, Prince.
Will you walk on ?

PAULO.

Nay, haste him not, Antonio.

ANTONIO.

How, Paulo, lingering still ?   Come, I excuse thee.
This fellow's service, Prince, is so devoted ;

Come, come, I have said go.   [BEPPO *laughs.*

                    Whose laugh is that ?
Is Beppo here ?

PAGE.

        I do not see him, seignior.

ANTONIO.

That was his laugh.   My gracious Prince, your
    pardon,
But you were saying——

BEPPO, *laughing again.*

        Man, don't you know me ?

ANTONIO.

Know you ?   Now by my dudgeon if I live
To doff this doublet I will deal you, sirrah——

PAULO.

Come, come, the Prince ! the Prince !

ANTONIO.

                    Prince me no more ;
I 've had enough of princes.

        [*Exeunt.   Enter* GIOVANNI *and* GINEVRA.

GINEVRA.

And you remember still ?

GIOVANNI.

            Ay, lady, still.

GINEVRA.

A face just lifted from the circling crowd
And straightway lost again like some white wave
Swallowed by sister billows ?

GIOVANNI.

Even so,

GINEVRA, *with agitation.*

And love me ?

GIOVANNI.

Love you ?   O that words, weak words,
Mere bubbles of the breath tossed out to die
On every wayward breeze that frets the air,
Are all I have to tell you, dear, how much.
Love you ?   My whole soul floats upon your smile
As on a restless sea.   I cannot breathe
My natural breath in your sweet atmosphere
But it does seem to catch a fairy fragrance.
Love you ?   My wild heart leaps unto my lips ;
I love you so I scarce can say I love you.

GINEVRA, *shrinking.*

O God ! and I——

GIOVANNI.

And you ?

GINEVRA, *advancing to the casement.*

Seignior, look forth !
Dost see yon orb of light that girt with power

Rides the still spaces of the firmament,
Queen-like within her golden chariot ?
One might in honor worship such a star
Shining supreme upon the front of night,
Nor bate him much from that high majesty
Of self-respect that makes a man a man.
But what of its reflection in the stream,
That puny brilliance which with borrowed gleam
Stares upward from the hollow of the wave
Soulless and unsubstantial ?   Lives there one
On all this round of earth could stoop so low
As to do homage there ?   Yet, gentle seignior,
The ideal you have loved is such a star,
I but the weak reflection.

GIOVANNI.

                         Say you so ?
Then are you heaven's high orb made low an
     sweet
For earthly service and companionship,
And I the wave which holds your beauty shrined
Deep in its cradling bosom.   Ah, Ginevra,
Too young to know that love asks small excuse
Of worthiness for loving, let your smile
But cross betimes my stern and iron path,
And I will ask no other light on earth
To guide my steps aright.   For where love shine
Ambition owns no pitfalls, fame no sting,
Nor is it in hard disappointment's power
To quite undo us.

GINEVRA.

Ah, it is too much !
You love me far too well.

GIOVANNI.

Ay, were my days
Hung upon sport and dalliance ; but with war
Sounding his eager clarion in my ear,
His sword within my hand, and on my brow
The shadow of the great *to do and be*
Which runs before high fame, 't is saving grace
To dote so well and fondly.   O sweet angel !
Beacon of light to my long-harassed soul,
What boon hath potent Fortune fair enough
To win thee from me.   When a dying wretch
Will yield the cup that bubbles to his lip
After long thirst and anguish, then will I
Yield thee and perish.   But you tremble, sweet one,
The envious night wind wooing your fair cheek
Hath chilled your gentle blood.   Let us pass on.

GINEVRA.

No, no, 't is nought.   I——[*aside*] O to hear such words,
And feel them strike my breast like blunted arrows.
[*They pass on.*

Enter LEON *and* BIANCA.

LEON.

He 's here.   But this same moment I perceived
His form glide through the porch.   If as I fear

He comes to mar the feast with jealous rage,
'T were fit some warning of the same were given
Unto my noble lord.   Where is he, lady ?

BIANCA.

Yonder, with his betrothed.   Ah, Seignior Leon,
I fear your words' effect.   He loves her truly,
And she—she might have peace had this young
    gallant
Kept himself hence awhile.

LEON.

                    That were to find
Judgment in youth and manhood's sternest virtue
Ruling th' unchastened spirit of a boy.
But to my task.   Pray heav'n I quit me of it
With wisdom and discretion.   [*Exit.*

BIANCA.

                    I will follow ;
Perchance my woman's wit may help the cause.
                                        [*Exit.*

Enter GIOVANNI *and* LEON.

GIOVANNI.

You think I am too happy ?

LEON.

                    Nay, my lord,
I think the maid too fair.   A love that hath
No surer basis than a winsome face
Crumbles too oft to ruin.

GIOVANNI.

So 't is said ;
But, Leon, hast thou loved ?

LEON.

Not yet, my lord.

GIOVANNI.

Then listen.   They who see her call her fair ;
Say her smile pleases ; that her voice is soft ;
Her cheek the home of blushes, light, and joy ;
Her glance a shifting glory ; and her brow
The throne of beauty and the seat of truth.
But as for me, I can see nought of this.
I do not know if she be fair or not.
A blind man just restored to light, I ween,
Would scarcely stop in looking at a rose
To say that it was beautiful.   I only know
Her glance is revelation, and her smile
A torturing delight.   Her slightest move
Wakes rapture in me.   When I look at her
I feel in that one instant all the reach
The human soul can scale in depth and height,
In ecstasy and pain ; so much I love her.

LEON.

Love ? love ? my lord has love ? he 's sure of it ?

GIOVANNI.

Sure of my love ?

LEON.

Sure of the lady, seignior ;
Women are so oft given to fickleness.

GIOVANNI.

Leon, dost see this sword ?   It was my grandsire's,
And on its very blade grim Honor sits
As on a throne.   I 'd rather wipe
Its score of deeds and old-time memories
Off in the base blood of a whining cur,
Than soil my lips with bandying doubts of her
Whom, loving, I would wed.

LEON.

My love for you
Led me too far, my lord.   I meant no evil.

GIOVANNI.

There, I believe it ; speak of it no more ;
You are my very friend ; yet hark you, Leon,
'T is easier for a man to bear all shame,
Anguish and wrong, than listen to a doubt
Urged 'gainst a well-beloved woman's honor.
Yet are you my own Leon.   Friend, your brow
Shows signs of watching.   Had you dreams last
     night ?

LEON.

Yes, I had dreams, but ask not what they were
Lest they should anger you.   They were of her.

GIOVANNI.

Of her—Ginevra ? You did dream of her
And never tell me, Leon ?

LEON.

Good my lord ;
It was of this I would have spoke when you——

GIOVANNI.

No more.   Tell me your dream.   What was it,
Leon ?

LEON.

My lord, I dreamed I saw her at the altar,
A glorious, smiling bride.

GIOVANNI.

Yes, yes.

LEON.

I dreamed
She was so beauteous that I stood and gazed
Long on her speaking face, unknowing why
My heart refused its joy, until I turned
My eyes in following hers upon her bridegroom,
And saw—well, well, ask me not whom I saw—
It was not thou.   O gentle seignior, pardon.

GIOVANNI.

Pardon for what ?   For an unhallowed dream,
Born of your restless fear ?   Good Leon, listen.

It is the fashion of our gallants here
To harp on woman's frailty and fondness ;
Until, to hear them talk, one scarce would think
God had reserved himself a single jewel
In his vast treasure-house of womankind,
Untarnished and unflawed.   This fashion, Leon,
Hath evil in it past the ill it does
To those we most should honor, for it leaves
A dark spot in the mind where doubt, once gen-
      dered,
Wallows for evermore.   I 'll none of it ;
And, therefore, though you dream me dreams of
      hell,
I 'll hold unto my faith in womankind
As I hold on to God.   The pure in heart
Have right to trust in others' purity.

                LEON, *aside.*

Ay, ay, 't is so.   What man will dare to tell him
That he who leans on fair Ginevra's faith
Leans to his fall.   Seignior, I say no more.
Before such trust Suspicion hides her face,
Abashed at her own daring.   [*Going.*
                              [*Enter* BIANCA.
                    Ah, Bianca,
My words have failed, may yours have better
      fortune.   [*Exit.*

              BIANCA, *aside.*

My words are tears ; what else befits the hour ?

GIOVANNI, *thoughtfully drawing his sword.*

I said it was my grandsire's ; I said well ;
I saw his cheek flush and the quick thrill run
The length of his man's frame—such virtue dwells
On the high front of fame to startle men.
Ah, noble sword, what fortune lies before thee
In my untutored hands ! Will high Renown
Leap with thy flash as in the days of yore ?
And proud-eyed Victory run to kiss thy edge
Before the day be done ? We may not know ;
We can but hope and trust.   [*Sees* BIANCA.
                   Ah, gracious lady,
Your pardon for my daring ! Naked steel
Hath little business here.

BIANCA.

                   True, true, then sheath it—
Nay, seal it to thy scabbard. Wrong and loss
Are not to be thus met.

GIOVANNI.

                   Wrong and loss ?

Enter at the back CAMILLO *and* GINEVRA *in tender
converse.*

BIANCA.

Ay, ay, look there, but do not draw your sword ;
Let Heav'n avenge thee here.   [*Exit.*

GIOVANNI.

What do I see ?
My brother — my betrothed — hand clasped in
    hand—
Face turned to face—his full of grief and worship,
While hers—[*staggering back*] O heav'n ! what is this
    doom I see
Shadowing upon me from the seat of bliss
I reckoned all my own !

GINEVRA *to* CAMILLO.

No more.   Since Fate
Has pledged me to your brother, speech twixt us
Is well-nigh treason.

CAMILLO.

Yet such speech must be.
I am no boy to yield my treasure up
Without an effort to arrest the hand
That seeks to rob me.   If Giovanni knew—

GIOVANNI, *coming forward.*

If ? Does he not ?   Can one stand witness here
And *not* know ?

GINEVRA.

Count Giovanni !
[*Turns to fly.*

GIOVANNI.

Stay ! a word
To make all sure.   Brother, is this fair woman,

Whom but a moment since I thought my own,
She whom you told me of a week agone ?

CAMILLO.

The same, alas !

GIOVANNI.

Not some fair semblance simply,
Like her in feature, form, or circumstance,
But she, herself, the rich Risifi's daughter ?

CAMILLO.

Ay, brother, she herself.

GIOVANNI.

Oh ! they spake well
Who said the brightest morns brought heaviest
days.
[*Turning towards her but not looking at her.*
Lady, you know this boy ; have seen him oft,
And mind his features well. Is it, then, he
Who holds the star, while I the weak reflection ?
If not, speak, speak, and I will risk my all
To make you mine indeed. [*A pause.*] Ye powers
that wait
On mortal souls, gird up my heart to bear
This heavy silence ! [*Another pause.*] What, quite
still ? No word,
No whisper light as air or dying breath,
To bid Giovanni hope ? Ah, well ; thus sinks
The ship full freighted in the hollow sea,
Leaving no sign behind !

CAMILLO.

Brother ?

GINEVRA.

Giovanni ?

GIOVANNI.

Lady, I ne'er have been a happy man.
Gaunt care and circumstance have warped my life
In youth's first prime.   If with the sight of thee
Some wandering beam of hope found passage
      through
Life's darkness to my heart, 't was God's good gift
Whose loss I 'll not bemoan.   If ye two love
Ye shall be happy.   It is not for me,
A man past youth's first flush, to coldly stand
A shadow on the threshold of your joy.

CAMILLO.

And thou ?

GIOVANNI.

And I ?   [*A pause.*
When in the heat of sounding battle-fields
A soldier stands, black danger in his path,
And in his hand the sword to make that danger
Shrink at his feet appalled, one does not ask
If joy or sorrow nerves the arm that wrests
Proud victory from the foe.   It is enough
The heart is steady and the arm is steel ;
High fame inquires no more.   O thou great Power
That broods above the smoky ranks of war,

To thee henceforth I dedicate my soul !
In thy huge volleyings hear the voice of love,
And from the blaze of thy high beacon fires
Snatch, like Prometheus, the living flame
To feed my soul anew.   While Honor calls,
Despair cries out in vain.   [*Rushes forth.*

[*Enter* RISIFI, *meeting him.   He is followed by*
OSALDI, ZENO, URBINO, *and others.*]

RISIFI.

Hold ! why this haste ?
And yon pert stripling by my daughter's side—
Who may he be, my lord ?

GIOVANNI, *returning.*

One who now holds
Right prior to me here.   My brother, seignior ;
The noblest of our race, a youth in whom
All truest virtues live, and furthermore
He whom high Heav'n ordains to wed your daughter.

RISIFI.

He ?   This slim boy ?   And you, Giovanni, you,
Who but an hour ago received her hand
From me in fair betrothal ?

GIOVANNI.

I am a soldier ;
The sweets of love and fair domestic joys
Are not for me.

RISIFI.

　　　　　　And by what right, my lord,
Do you adjudge them with my daughter here
Unto this stripling, though he be your brother?
Is he by chance, for all his beardless lip,
Elder than you in years?

GIOVANNI.

　　　　No.

RISIFI.

　　　　　　　　Then, by heaven,
I know no law or human or divine
That can ordain him to espouse my child,
Betrothed but now to thee.

CAMILLO.

　　　　　　　Yet is there one.

RISIFI.

Ha! would'st *thou* speak?

CAMILLO.

　　　　　　A law which none may break,
In this rough world of few and fleeting joys,
Without such penalty as Nature asks
From those who cross her will—the law of Love.

RISIFI.

Love! 'T is the prate of fools. I know not love;
Nor does my daughter, hedged about and in

As she hath been from earliest infancy ;
Or, if by chance the watchfulness of years
Has been in vain, and by some loop-hole small
The Devil has crept in, what pow'r hath that
To make me yield my will.   I 'd have her princess,
And princess shall she be, or die a maid.

CAMILLO.

O mad ambition !

GINEVRA.

Struggle not with it ;
Our doom is fixed, all words will be in vain.

ZENO *to* GIOVANNI.

You are a prince ; take that which is thine own
And cease this foolish strife.

GIOVANNI.

It may not be.
Seignior Risifi, on thy yea or nay
Rests this young maiden's life.   For love is life,
And loss of love is death.   Is her sweet being
Less to your fatherhood than hope of rank ?
Her happiness and honor, peace and joy,
Smaller than satisfaction of a wish
Never called holy, never born in heaven,
But gendered in the bosom of that angel
Who sold himself for pride ?   I cannot think it ;
The strong surprise of this quick change has turned
Your fatherhood awry.   A moment's thought
Will bring its own repentance.

RISIFI.

　　　　　　　　Say you so ?
Then know you not Risifi.　Sooner far
The sun shall turn its back upon the east
And trample out its own refulgent steps
Than I yield up my purpose.　But enough !
If one short hour has wearied your young blood
Of charms once thought so bounteous and rare,
Leave her and go thy way ;　I urge no man
Against his will ;　but talk not to my age
Of what its duties are, nor in the shame
Of your own treason, fetch this stripling here
To gloss o'er your default.

GIOVANNI.

　　　　　　　　Seignior, my griefs
Needed no added sting.　If she were free,
Naught that the world affords of pomp or power
Could win her from my arms.　But she 's not free,
And I who hold that honor's springs lie deep
Beneath all selfish yearning, yield her up
To joys more truly hers.

RISIFI.

　　　　　　　　'T is well ;　the son
Of Uzzi's lord will thank you.

GIOVANNI.

　　　　　　　　Uzzi ?

RISIFI.

Ay,

Dids't think such charms as hers had tipped the
  scale
Against your pride alone ?

CAMILLO.

But Uzzi, seignior ?
It is a villain brood.

RISIFI.

It is a lord's.

GIOVANNI.

O this is horrible !

CAMILLO.

Most horrible.
Can'st look upon this sacrifice, Giovanni ?

GIOVANNI.

I ?

CAMILLO.

She is young ; her years lie long before her ;
Save her from this hard fate and take my thanks.

GIOVANNI.

What, would you tempt me with that thought
  again ?

CAMILLO.

'T is no temptation, 't is thy rightful due.
Whate'er may chance, I ne'er may hope to wed her,
Then why not thou?

GIOVANNI.

True, true, then why not I?

URBINO *to* RISIFI.

He yields, Risifi; urge him but a jot
And all is yours again.

RISIFI.

I urge no man
Against his pleasure. If my daughter's charms
Lack power to hold him to his plighted vow,
Shall words of mine prevail?

GIOVANNI.

O God! 't is hard.

RISIFI.

And is that all, my lord?

GIOVANNI, *with effort.*

All, all, alas!

RISIFI.

Then are we quits. Urbino, to the doors!
Let our guests know that in a fortnight hence
We celebrate our union with Count Uzzi.

GINEVRA.

O no, no, no, that were to die indeed !
                    [*Falls at* GIOVANNI's *feet.*
Save me, Giovanni, save me from a fate
Too dreadful for my strength.

GIOVANNI.

                    What ! do *you* plead ?
O heaven, this is too much !   Rise, lady, rise,
I may not see thee thus.

GINEVRA.

                    Nor may I rise
Until you grant my suit.

GIOVANNI.

                    And what is that ?

GINEVRA, *timidly.*

Most graciously to wed me, seignior.

GIOVANNI.

                    Wed thee ?
O God ! O God ! And could'st thou wed me, lady,
Be my pledged wife and not behold in dreams
The younger, brighter, dearer face of him
Who stands there in despair ?   Look at him, lady,
Mark well his face, his beauty, and his love,
And tell me, by the heavens which bend above us,
Could you do this ?

GINEVRA, *wildly.*

I know not ; ask me not.
My thoughts are all in tumult.

GIOVANNI.

Thou could'st not ;
I see it in thy fond and failing eye
Which droops before his gaze.   Would'st have me
    wed
The lover of another ?   Friends, farewell ;
I have no other business in this place.   [*Going.*

RISIFI.

And now to fresh betrothals !   Sound the lute
And let the dance whirl on.
        [*Trumpet heard without.*
Ha ! what is that ?
        [*Enter Messenger.*

MESSENGER.

A summons from the Duke to Count Giovanni,
Captain by right of birth and monies promised
Unto the cause of war.

[GIOVANNI *advances, takes the paper offered, is about to
    open it, but suddenly stops, looks at* RISIFI, *and
    drops it.*]

RISIFI.

        By monies promised !
My lord, have you such monies ?

GIOVANNI.

No, seignior, no.
I had forgot to whom I was beholden
For ev'n the chance to die.

RISIFI, *pointing to the packet.*

Then let it lie
Till Uzzi comes to lift it.

[GIOVANNI *starts forward, but instantly recovers
himself.*]

GIOVANNI.

Nay, 't is true.
My captaincy is gone with this child's love,—
All, all in one quick breath.

ZENO.

Nor that alone ;
Thy house, thy father, thy young brother too,
Sink in the ruin with thee.

OSALDI.

Ah, 't is so, 't is so,
Our house is fallen !   All my hopes but served
To lift its misery plainer into view
For all men's mockery.

ZENO.

Draw thy sword, Giovanni,—
Thy grandsire's sword that was to carve our way
To reinstatement.   Can'st thou look on it

And not recall the hopes its mem'ries gave,
The day you drew it first ?

GIOVANNI.

Zeno, no more.

CAMILLO.

And this dear maiden whom you love so well.
Look at her, brother ; can you see such beauty
Flung to an Uzzi's keeping?

GIOVANNI.

Cease, O cease !
Man's heart can bear no more.   Whate'er betides,
Uzzi stays hence.   Forth to the courier, man ;
Bid him acquaint the Duke that e'er to-morrow
His captain will be there.

ZENO.

I live again.

OSALDI.

And I, who thought to leave my aged bones
Upon this hostile floor.

GIOVANNI.

And thou, Camillo ?

CAMILLO.

My highest love cries *Ay*, howe'er my heart
Bleeds at its heavy loss.

GIOVANNI.

Brother, I love thee.
Remember this when from the field of war
Ginevra's bridegroom brings the bays of fame
To crown his wreath of love.

CAMILLO.

I will remember.
[GIOVANNI *turns to depart.*

RISIFI.

Whither would'st go, my lord?

GIOVANNI.

To seek a priest
Who 'll bind this knot at once.

RISIFI.

I 'll seek him, seignior;
Thy place is at her side. [*Exit.*

GIOVANNI *to* GINEVRA.

Sweet, may I take it?
[*She gives him her hand.*
Thanks, dearest lady; may the happy man
Who calls thee wife love thee but half as well
As he you honor thus. Father, your blessing.

OSALDI.

You have it, son, poured out as full and free
As though you were the only hope I had.
And this thy top-most hour.

GIOVANNI.

Brother—but no !
Confession must be made ere marriage vows,
And lo ! here comes the priest.
                    [*Enter* RISIFI *with a priest.*
                    Ah ! holy father,
Wilt shrive me ere you wed me ?

PRIEST.

Gladly, son.
[GIOVANNI, *lifting the curtain from before a
            small closet.*]
In, then, and may high Heav'n rain dews of joy
Upon the hearts I leave here.
                    [*Exit slowly, looking at* GINEVRA

LEON.

What means this shudder ?
I feel as though mine eyes had seen his ghost.

ZENO.

And I ; yet all is well.   'T is but his grief
At robbing his young brother of the love
So suited to his years.

OSALDI.

O Zeno, Zeno !
How like his mother did he look but now.
Should there be aught amiss !

RISIFI, *aside.*

I wished it, yet
My blood runs cold within me.

GINEVRA *to* BIANCA.

Were it wrong
To cast one farewell glance at him I loved
Before this duty claimed me ?

BIANCA.

It were not wise
But——. [*A cry within.*] What is that ?
[*Enter the priest hurriedly.*

PRIEST.

Death ! death ! The noble count
Hath turned his sword against his own brave heart,
And all is over.

OSALDI.

O my mastering fears !

LEON, *rushing and dragging aside the curtain from
before the closet.*

My lord ?

CAMILLO.

Giovanni ?

OSALDI.

Ah, my son, my son !

GIOVANNI.

Hush, it is done.   My sword has cut the knot
That baffled all our skill.   Camillo, brother,
You love this gentle child?

CAMILLO.

I ! O thou know'st.

GIOVANNI.

Then take her hand in thine.   I 'm dying, brother,
And you are now the heir.   But these have said
Osaldi's heir should wed Risifi's daughter ;
Dost comprehend me now ?

CAMILLO.

O brother ! brother !

GIOVANNI.

No words,—your hands—thine, lady,—thine, Ca-
millo—
What, have I lost my sense ? I do not feel
The touch of thine, Camillo.

CAMILLO.

'T is too awful.
Perhaps some future day—

GIOVANNI.

No, now.

RISIFI.

Give him thy hand.
Would 'st kill him twice and make the girl a widow
Before her sixteenth year ?

[CAMILLO *gives his hand.*

GIOVANNI.

So, you will love each other.
Friends, lift me up.   A light, there on her face !
I 'd see her once again.   So, so.   [*Sinks back.*

LEON.

O live, Giovanni !

GIOVANNI *starting to his feet and standing.*

No, die !   [*Falls back dead.*

THE END.